Also by Karin Tetlow and Tessa Guze
Harry The Carousel Horse

Jumping Horse Press
Philadelphia, PA
www.jumpinghorsepress.com

ISBN 978-0-615-75585-4

Harry
Goes Rowing

Dedicated to horse lovers and rowers everywhere

Harry
Goes Rowing

Written by Karin Tetlow   Illustrated by Tessa Guze

Harry was a white horse who lived on a carousel. He and all the other horses had started rowing.

A special Coach was training them to compete in a famous race called the Head of the Horse River.

Harry loved wearing his red and blue striped unisuit. He imagined winning a gold medal!

One morning the Coach asked Harry to be the cox.
The cox steers the boat and shouts directions through a loudspeaker called
a cox box so that all the rowers can hear.

Harry did not want to be the cox.
He was smaller than the other horses, and he guessed that the Coach wanted
him only because he could fit into the very small cox's space in the boat.
"I want to row," he said to himself.

Knowing that he had to follow the Coach's orders, he sat in the boat. But he could not concentrate and shouted "Ready...row" when he meant to say "Let it run" or stop rowing.

"You will learn," said the Coach. "But you must pay attention."

That night Harry forgot to set his alarm clock and was late for the practice.

All the boats had left. Even the launch the Coach drove had gone. Harry stood on the dock and watched the geese. After a while he slowly walked back to the carousel.

On the way he passed the Cosmic Café where the Biglin brothers were having breakfast. They were famous rowers who had won many races. "Cheer up Harry," they called out.

But Harry didn't want to cheer up. He wanted to row.

That night Harry had a dream. He travelled across the ocean and visited his friend Will. Will was a very old white horse who lived on a hill and smiled at the beautiful shapes in the cornfields below.

"What's the matter?" asked Will.
"I want to be on the team, but I don't want to be the cox," answered Harry. "The Coach only wants me because I'm small and can fit into the tiny cox space."

Will was silent for long time. Finally he spoke.
"Many years go, I was in an important race. We were faster than the other boats. But we lost the race. Do you know why? The cox steered us off the racecourse. We crossed the line of buoys that mark where we were supposed to row.

"It's the cox who is in charge, and he or she wins or loses the race."

Harry thought about this.
"You mean that he wants me because he thinks I can be in charge, that I can steer and tell the rowers how to row? Not just because I am small?"

"Exactly," said Will.

The next day Harry arrived early at the river. He shooed the geese into the water and swept the dock. He said a bright "Good Morning" to the Coach and apologized for missing the practice.

The Coach nodded and gave Harry the cox box.

Weeks passed. The team practiced and practiced. Harry concentrated and learned when to call "Power ten," the signal for the rowers to row extra hard for ten strokes.

Finally, they were at the Head of the Horse River.
The weather was terrible. It was cold and windy. The
rain was pouring down in torrents.

"Oars out," shouted Harry. "Tails in."
All eight horses pulled in their tails.
"Count down when ready," he shouted next.
"One," "Two," "Three," "Four," "Five," "Six," "Seven,"
"Eight," said each horse in turn.
"Row," ordered Harry.

The team rowed upstream to the start of the race.

They turned around and waited for their turn, watching
the white caps on the rough water.

The starter called out, "Carousel Crew, Ready...row."

And off they went down the river. Harry steered under
several bridges and then took a sharp left turn, taking
care not to cross the buoy line.

"Power ten," he called.

They passed a boat. They passed another boat.

The wind blew harder, and waves of water slurped into the boat.

The boat sank lower and lower in the water.

"Keep rowing!" Harry shouted.
They kept rowing until the boat disappeared beneath them.

"Swim with the boat!" Harry screamed.
Harry and the eight horses swam as hard as they could, pushing the boat across the finish line by the Viking statue.

The buzzer buzzed. The race was over.

After helping the horses pull the boat out of the water, the Coach read the results of the race on his cell phone. A big grin appeared on his face.

He looked at them all and proudly announced, "You had the fastest time! You won!"

The next day at the carousel Harry and his teammates wore their gold medals.

Photo by Edmund W. Golaski

Real Life Notes

Harry lives on the carousel at the Mall in Washington D.C. Once upon a time he was shiny white, but now he is painted in different colors like his friends, the other horses. Behind the saddle of each horse is a brass plate engraved with the name of a U.S. state. The name on Harry's brass plate may be where you live.

The fall is head racing season where crews compete against the clock over a three-mile-plus course. Among the best known races in the U.S. are the Head of the Charles on the Charles River in Boston, Mass., and the Head of the Schuylkill on the Schuylkill River in Philadelphia, Pa. Bad weather and negotiating the course with its many bridges are some of the challenges.

Rowers share the river with Canadian geese. Some geese lay their eggs high above the river on bridge abutments while their mates noisily keep guard in the water below. When they are not swimming and flying like bullets over rowing crews, the geese waddle on the banks eating grass. They also like to visit the boathouses. Rowers have to sweep up after them.

Will is the two-hundred-year-old old Alton Barnes white horse carved out of chalk in Wiltshire, England. He looks down on the mysterious crop circles that appear every year in ever more complex designs.

Known as the Viking, the statue of Thorfinn Karlsefni, Icelandic explorer and father of the first known European child born in the New World, marks the finish line for head races on the Schuylkill River in Philadelphia, Pa. He was painted Phillies-red after the Philadelphia Phillies won the 2008 World Series.

John and Barney Biglin were professional rowers from New York City forever re-membered in Thomas Eakins' paintings.* In the famous paired-oared match race on the Schuylkill River in Philadelphia, Pa., in May 1872, they beat the Pittsburgh crew by steering a shorter course. Rough water, high winds and heavy rain delayed the start of the five-mile race but crowds of Philadelphians stayed to cheer and bet successfully on the outcome.

CPSIA information can be obtained at www.ICGtesting.com
Printed in the USA
LVIW01n2317191016
509514LV00005B/10

* 9 7 8 0 6 1 5 7 5 5 8 5 4 *